The
Fireplace

GL Westover

11-15-11

The
Fireplace

WHERE USUAL & UNUSUAL THINGS HAPPEN

written by
G.R. Westover

TATE PUBLISHING *& Enterprises*

Published by Tate Publishing & Enterprises, LLC
127 E. Trade Center Terrace | Mustang, Oklahoma 73064 USA
1.888.361.9473 | www.tatepublishing.com

Tate Publishing is committed to excellence in the publishing industry. The company reflects the philosophy established by the founders, based on Psalm 68:11,
"The Lord gave the word and great was the company of those who published it."

Book design copyright © 2011 by Tate Publishing, LLC. All rights reserved.
Cover and interior design by Chris Webb
Illustrations by Justin Stier

Published in the United States of America

ISBN: 978-1-61777-569-7
1. Juvenile Fiction / Family / Multigenerational
2. Juvenile Fiction / Historical / United States / General
11.11.07

Dedication

This book is dedicated with love to Jamie, Craig, Justin, Amber, and Aaron, the best grandkids you could ever want. It also is dedicated to their spouses, Mike, Jenny, Michelle, and Martin. The dedication follows through to the great grandkids, Katie, Anna, Aiden, and Mason (who has gone to live in heaven). It is dedicated to my husband, Fred. We have shared over fifty years of love. It is also dedicated to our son, Fred, Jr. and to our daughter, Kathy, and their spouses, Sandy and Rich. Each one makes my life and helps me tremendously in so many different ways. I hope this book will be an inspiration to all who read it. You should pursue your "hopes" and dreams. God bless.

Acknowledgments

I want to thank God for inspiring me to write this book and giving me the courage to submit it. Thanks to Tate for publishing it. A big thank you goes to Janey for her encouraging words. Thank you to Ron and Alice, for their friendship and having the fireplace that helped create the idea of this book.

One

Just north of the Mason-Dixon Line on a dreary, Sunday afternoon, five cousins could never suspect the amazing adventure that was to unfold in their lives.

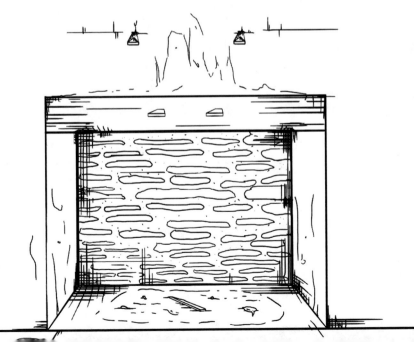

The kids, along with their parents, spent almost every other Sunday with their Poppy and Grammy Nelson. Marie, fifteen, had always been the "mother hen" type. She still enjoyed (sometimes) being with the younger kids. Allen, thirteen, was as big a tease as one could imagine. What he didn't think of now, he did later. Leigh, ten, always had a smile on her face. She was very much the daredevil. Their parents were Edward and Fay Nelson. Richard, eleven, was tall and thin. He seemed to grow inches overnight. He was usually the quiet one. Jay, seven, enjoyed imitating everything the other kids did. He was usually happy go lucky. Their parents were Lynn and R. J. Hendricks.

On this rainy day, while the adults were discussing plans for celebrating America's bicentennial next year, the kids decided to play hide and seek in the basement. It was an ordinary basement for an old house. Part of it had been modernized with a furnace and a sink, stove, refrigerator and dishwasher. It was used mostly in canning season. The part that was not finished had a very unique structure in it. A huge wooden fireplace was located right in the center of the north wall. There was a section in this part that still had a dirt floor.

The cousins knew the fireplace had not been in use for years and years. It was hard to imagine a fire in a wooden fireplace, but there were definite signs of usage——the hooks for the kettles, the darkened wood from the fires, and the ever so slight smell of smoke. One other time when they were down there they saw evidence of some crumbling stone work.

Marie was to be "it." While she waited, the others crept down the steps, trying not to giggle. Once the cousins got in this unfinished part of the basement, they were less afraid of Marie hearing them. They talked about several good spots that had worked for them in prior games. They knew Marie was a good "finder." She usually discovered them in no time at all.

Allen said, "I'll climb on top of one of these beams." Richard said, "I'll stand behind this large support post and just move around as she gets near." Leigh said, "I have a great idea. Let's go up the fireplace chimney." Jay said, "That is a great idea. Let's do it." Richard said, "Don't forget about the loose piece of concrete that fell out of there that one time we were down here." They had to make a decision quickly, as their time was running out. Finally they decided to try to get up the chimney of the fireplace.

They helped each other up until they found a foothold inside the chimney. Then Allen was pulled up by the others. It was a difficult job, but once they were in position, it was the perfect hiding spot.

Soon Marie would be coming down the steps, calling, "Ready or not, here I come!" Sure enough, they had no sooner gotten Allen up and out of sight before she was down there.

She looked everywhere, even crawled up a ladder to see if any of them were hiding on the big beams. She reached and looked around the support posts. She searched for a good five minutes before finally giving up. It was a good thing, too.

The cousin's arms and legs were tiring from holding themselves in place.

As they were making their way out of the chimney, laughing and bragging about their good hiding place, a couple of big bricks dislodged. One almost hit Leigh on the head. Jay said, "I hope we aren't going to get in trouble for this."

They decided to push the bricks back in place by lifting up Richard, who was pretty tall. As he was trying to put the last brick in place, something was keeping it from fitting. He put his hand in the opening to pull out what he figured was loose mortar. He brushed it out, and the cousins that were holding him up almost dropped him. He managed to quickly get the brick in place.

They all stared in amazement after Richard had been lowered. His hands seemed to be glowing gold. Jay almost started to cry. He was really scared. Then they all realized the stuff he had brushed out was sprinkled over them. Some of it lay on the floor of the fireplace. A goldish glow was emitting everywhere the stuff had touched.

Marie gasped and tried to say something, but nothing would come out. Allen said, "Let's put some dirt off the floor on it to get it off or cover it up."

Leigh just laughed and said, "Oh, he is playing a trick on us."

Richard said, "No, I'm not! What can this stuff be?"

Marie finally found her voice and said, "It must have been a hiding place for someone's gold." They all agreed that was probably what it was. Richard said, "But, why is it glowing?" Nobody had an answer.

Richard used some dirt to wipe off his hands. Everyone was helping to put dirt on wherever they saw the glow, including the floor of the fireplace.

They all knew their parents would be wondering about them and telling them it would soon be time to leave. They made plans to not say anything about their find to anyone. On their next visit, they would investigate further.

Two

Two weeks passed before they got together again at their grandparent's house. They could hardly wait until dinner was over so they could go to the basement and discuss the situation.

Marie had spent the two weeks researching at the library as to what could possibly emit a golden glow. She did not have any success. Allen was confident he knew what caused it. He thought iron, not gold, had been long stored in the chimney wall. When it was disturbed, a chemical reaction occurred between the iron, heat and some other element he hadn't figured out yet. Richard and Jay had discussed the

mystery at length. They were convinced the glow was caused by gold that had been hidden there for a long, long time. They figured that when the gold came in contact with the normal atmosphere of the basement, along with the elements created by pollution from the fireplace, the gold just sort of dissolved into a glow. Or, it had disintegrated with age, into very small particles that only looked like it was glowing. Leigh thought the glow was from an outer space alien that had been discovered and killed by a previous owner.

As the cousins neared the fireplace, there was nothing to be seen. They were totally bewildered. Each began to wonder if their imaginations had just run wild. Then they decided it was time to talk to the adults. They decided Marie should be the one to tell them.

When they got upstairs, they were glad to see everyone was sitting around the table. The adults looked at the kids, knowing something was going on. Marie quickly spoke, asking her dad and aunt, "Do either of you ever remember any unusual happenings in the basement while you were growing up?" Neither Edward nor Lynn could recall anything. The grandparents said lately they both had heard noises down there. Each had gone down to check, but found absolutely nothing, other than some crumbly mortar. They figured an elusive mouse or a bird had found its way inside. The question sure did peak their curiosity, though.

Poppy Nelson asked, "What is going on and why are you asking these questions?"

Marie said, "We have something to show and discuss with you by the wooden fireplace." So, down they all went.

As they gathered around the fireplace, Marie told them what had happened. Of course, the adults were skeptical. They tried to get the kids to admit making it all up. Finally, after much re-telling of the story, the grownups were convinced that the kids were telling them the truth as they remembered it. The fireplace was checked where they thought the loose brick had been. There was nothing but a very, very slight glow in the dirt. There was no substance to it, just the glow. They had almost missed it because it was so minute. Everyone searched diligently for any other signs of the glow. None could be found.

After discussing what could be the cause, without being able to reach any reasonable conclusion or solution, Grammy Nelson said, "We will go to the courthouse and dig through records of previous owners. That might lead to finding an answer." Poppy Nelson said, "I'll talk to some of the real old timers around town. Someone might be able to shed some light on this strange phenomenon."

In their probing, they were careful not to reveal why they were just now starting to seek information on the history of the house.

At the courthouse, Grammy Nelson found out the house had been built in 1781. It had housed some pretty influential people over the years.

Poppy Nelson had this to report. He said, "When I was getting my hair cut, the conversation got around to our house. A new customer, who was listening intently to our discussion, said he had recently moved to this area. He added that he was a descendent of someone who had once lived in our house. After a little probing, I found out his ancestor was a Dora Jacobs who was married to a Reuben Taylor. As I could hardly wait to hear what he had to say, I asked him if he would mind going to the nearby diner to get better acquainted and to hear more of this ancestor. He agreed and after some small talk, this is the tale he told that had been passed down through the generations."

Three

In 1862, during the Civil War, a family named Taylor occupied the house.

Even though the Taylors did not agree with slavery, they felt the war was more the result of pig-headed minds on both sides that wanted to control the agricultural and industrial commodities. When asked to become part of a group to help slaves find freedom further north, Mr. Taylor said yes. Being so close to Maryland, the danger would be very real, as there were more southern sympathizers than northern.

A secret room would have to be built in the basement. A perfect spot was by the wooden fireplace. Heat from it would penetrate the walls to help keep the hidden people warm during cool nights. The slaves were brought in on hay wagons, well hidden by the loose hay. They stayed on the wagons in the barn until late at night. Then they were taken, one by one, to the secret room. When they were all there, usually about four, food cooked in the big, iron kettle was given to them along with pails of water. It was used for drinking and washing up a little. A privy had also been built as an attachment to the barn. They could get to it through a disguised door built in the barn wall.

When curious neighbors asked why he had constructed a second privy so close to the barn, he said, "I spend so much time in that barn doing blacksmithing, woodworking and tending the animals. It just makes common sense to have one there instead of having to traipse across the yard in all kinds of weather."

Needless to say, the farmer and his family were petrified the first few times the hay wagon arrived. The Taylor family consisted of John, Cora, three sons, Reuben, age fifteen, Daniel, age thirteen, Matthew, age ten, and two daughters, Lucy, age eleven, and Rachel, age seven. They all worked very hard to keep their secret.

Mr. Taylor would take a completed piece of furniture or some repaired iron items into town. There he would stop to visit in the general store. The owner, Mr. Jacobs, was his contact. During the small-talk conversations, messages were relayed by a code that the two had devised. A nod to the left would mean an attack was planned in a certain area, two nods would mean the north was advancing toward a rebel stronghold. A brief handshake would mean a hay wagon was on its way. A vigorous handshake would mean the slaves were on their way north. It was quite ingenious in its simplicity.

During this time, a friendship developed between a couple of the slave children, whose names were James, thirteen, and Ruby, eight, and the Taylor children. The slave children were delayed from leaving due to a hold up of some sort at the end of their journey.

They all decided to meet or contact each other somehow some way at some point in the future.

The Taylor children tried to live as normal as most other children during this tumultuous time. Reuben, being the eldest helped his father a lot. He became smitten with the store owner's daughter. Her name was Dora and she was fourteen. He found every opportunity to go into town with his pa.

On one occasion, while he was with Dora, he let slip about James and Ruby. Of course, being very inquisitive (to the point of being called nosy by her friends and family), she had to know everything. She asked Reuben, "How old are they? Why didn't you tell me about them before? Where will they go? Where did they come from? And, I want to meet them! When will you arrange it?" Reuben swore her to secrecy before caving in to her pressure and answering her questions. She was so insistent and persuasive, he said, "I'll think of some way to make it happen, but you have to be patient. I'll let you know the plan the next time I come to town."

Reuben was now totally terrified. He was terrified his father would wallop him for letting out their secret, terrified the authorities would find out, arrest them all and hang them for treason, terrified that his brothers and sisters would find out and feel they could tell their friends. But mostly he was terrified that his romance would be done for if he didn't figure out some way to let Dora meet James and Ruby.

Before he could make that next trip, James and Ruby, along with the other concealed slaves, were secreted out to finish their journey.

Reuben was relieved, but didn't know how Dora would take this news. He didn't need to worry. The war had ended.

Mr. Taylor and his family were jubilant, even though he had tired of his dual role. He was proud of being able to help the slaves secure their chance for freedom and happiness. He firmly believed no person should be in bondage to another.

They all went into town to hear the latest news. Reuben was anxious to talk to Dora. She was happy to see him. She was disappointed that she had not gotten to meet James and Ruby. Reuben said, "We have made a pact to try to contact each other sometime in the future." She said, "I can't explain it. I just do not know why I feel so drawn to these two. I only know that at some point, I'll make their acquaintance."

Four

The years passed with many changes occurring throughout the land.

Daniel, Matthew, and Lucy Taylor got married and moved away. Reuben married Dora. Rachel married a cousin of Dora's, named Charles. They were never blessed with children, but sure did dote on their nephew and niece, after they were born.

Reuben and Dora lived in the farmhouse with his parents, after getting married. Shortly afterward, his pa was taken by a bad fever. Cora was devastated. She said, "Without my John, I don't think I can bear life." Reuben tried to console his ma. He said, "Time will help. And besides, your future grandchildren will need you and your loving guidance." It was not to be, though. Cora just lost her will to live. She never even got to see her first grandchild, John, who was born shortly after her death.

Despite the pain of losing both John and Cora, Reuben and Dora found much joy in their growing family. Two years after John was born Rebekah arrived. They told the children, even before they were old enough to understand, what special grandparents they would have had.

Dora and Reuben spent much time by the wooden fireplace. Even though the secret passageway had been sealed off, the memories were still there. They talked often of James and Ruby. During the winter, especially when Rachel and Charles came over, they would have popcorn and retell all the old stories. The fireplace seemed to be the focal point of their daily living. Dora would sit by it to do her mending, baby rocking, contemplating, and meditating.

By 1890, the gold fever was hitting the country hard. Although Reuben was forty-three, he felt his family should take the chance and go to the gold fields. He secretly wrote the territorial governor of Alaska asking for information.

One evening as the two of them set around the fireplace, Reuben cleared his throat to get her attention. He said, "I think we should all go to Alaska and try our luck at finding gold." Needless to say, Dora who knew that something was on his mind, was certainly not expecting that statement. After the initial shock, she said, "Reuben, you know I love you and trust you, but Alaska——gold! Have you considered all that would be involved?"

He reassured her, "I have not suggested this without careful consideration of all the possible complications." He shared the governor's letter with her.

She still was not convinced, but said, "I love you and if this is what you really want, the children and I will follow you."

When they told John, who was seven, and Rebekah, who was five, what they had decided, John became really excited. Rebekah was too young to understand, but she was caught up in all their excitement.

Reuben and Dora went to see Rachel and Charles to break the news to them. Leaving them was one of the great sorrows they faced. What a surprise it was to them when Charles said, "This is totally amazing news. We have been discussing this very same venture." Dora and Rachel started to cry. Their emotions were certainly being pushed to the limit. Charles said, "How soon would you be leaving? I will need a couple of months to close out my business dealings."

Reuben said, "We will need to leave as quickly as possible. The weather conditions could be dangerous and change without much warning."

Reuben was able to settle all affairs and arrange train tickets very quickly.

The family was able to leave within two weeks after having the conversation with Charles and Rachel. They would follow as soon as they could arrange all their business dealings.

Five

The train ride was exciting for everyone. When they got to Skagway, they purchased a wagon, some mules and a lot of supplies. They had been told the Canadian authorities required food and equipment to last up to one year.

Although they had heard stories of little communities starting up all over the place, they had no idea what to really expect. Reuben said, "Wherever 'fate' leads us, that's where we will set up camp.

After traveling along the regular path for days, Dora spotted a little stream. It was a beautiful place and it seemed to beckon her. After looking all around and seeing no other prospectors, Reuben said, "I guess you have found our spot. We'll set up here."

In the next few days, they did discover about half a dozen people working the stream.

Reuben had fashioned his own type of pan for sifting. It was a little different from others he had seen. There were two screens. The larger one on top would catch the nuggets while the much finer screen would catch the small particles. His thinking was that the finer gold would add up to enough for their living expenses. And, of course, the bigger nuggets would make them rich.

After working the stream for almost two weeks, Reuben had found a handful of nuggets. He took them to the nearest assay office, about ten miles away. The nuggets were worth almost twenty dollars. It cost him five dollars for the assaying and to stake and register his claim for that particular spot, which Dora had already dubbed "Hope."

They all worked very hard. When it was time for meals, Dora and Rebekah would stop panning and prepare lunch or supper. For breakfast they all just ate leftover hard tack and drank strong coffee.

There were not many women in the area. Most of the sourdoughs, as the prospectors were now being called, would take turns fixing the meals, while the others would stay in the stream. Over time, after becoming friends with some of them, it was suggested that Dora, with Rebekah's help, might want to do their cooking and washing. That way they could all stay out and pan.

This arrangement really worked out well. They paid in hard money. Dora would not take any gold. She figured this way the prospectors could see their cache keep building rather than taken away. Each small nugget was like a piece of their soul.

A trip back to Circle City was discussed. Some supplies needed replenishing and they were also anxious for word of Charles and Rachel.

Before the final arrangements for the trip were made, a peddler came through with supplies. He had seen a need to go around camps and provide, for a good profit, the depleted supplies. This would enable prospectors to keep working the streams.

Dora was able to get most of the things that were on her list. She also requested certain items the next time he was to come through. She asked, "Did you happen to hear any news of a man and woman trying to find us, the Taylors?"

She could hardly believe it when he said, "Yes, they should be only a couple of days behind me. They were getting supplies when I started out on this run."

Dora couldn't wait to tell Reuben and the children. Rebekah was so excited she couldn't keep her eyes off the road leading to the stream. She wanted to be the first to spot her aunt and uncle. She missed them very much.

When they finally arrived it was John who saw them. He had walked along the stream and was visiting with a boy who was about his own age. They were talking about a favorite fishing spot. It had provided some excellent meals. Just as John turned to head back to the camp, Charles and Rachel came along. He had grown so much, Rachel hardly recognized him.

They all stayed up late talking about the hardships both families had encountered in their traveling to get there. When Reuben and family left, they traveled by train from Baltimore to Lincoln, Nebraska. From there they took a stagecoach to Seattle. A boat then took them to Skagway. There they purchased mules, a wagon, and some necessary clothing, such as heavy, woolen underwear and socks, mackinaw coats and pants, rubber boots, rubber overcoats, light underwear, sweaters, and blankets. They also bought flour, beans, dried fruit, dried beef, coffee, and some salt pork. They had been told the other food supplies could be purchased when they got closer to their destination.

The entire trip went rather smoothly, despite some of their traveling companions. One fellow went off his head and tried to kill his wife. He kept ranting that it was all her fault that they left their comfortable home to go on this god-forsaken trip. Then another woman gave birth early. She and the baby had to be left at a stagecoach inn. She was on her way to meet her husband. A message was to be delivered to him if he could be found.

Charles and Rachel traveled a different route. They went over the Rockies by wagon. An unexpected, blinding snowstorm stopped them in their tracks. They were completely isolated for three days. When they had all but given up, a traveling parson helped their small party to find the trail again. Finally just getting to the Canadian border, was a big relief.

That is, until they found out what supplies they would have to have before going any further. Also, the huge distance that still lay between them and Circle City, Alaska. Needless to say, they were very discouraged.

After finding a place to rent for a few days, they enjoyed a real bath and sleeping in a bed. The room was above a saloon that was run by a woman named Martha. She took them under her wing, steering them clear of shysters and cheaters. She said Rachel reminded her of herself when she had made the trip in 1880. Her husband had owned this saloon, when he was killed in a robbery attempt. She had no desire to return to her hometown in Ohio. The saloon seemed the perfect place for her to make her living. She wasn't particularly proud of some things she had done, but her heart was in the right place. When people like Rachel and Charles happened by and she could help, it made her life worthwhile.

The supplies they would need to finish their trip seemed never ending. Martha told them of the store owner who was most honest. They followed her advice and went to place their order. They would need two wagons, a driver for the second one, six mules, lots of woolen clothing, blankets, cotton and woolen underwear, flour, bacon, dried beans, rice, cornmeal, rolled oats, coffee, tea, sugar, honey, dried fruits, salt, condensed milk, candles, soap, matches, medical supplies. They also bought some dried beef and dried salt pork. They needed rubber for mending, needles, threads, boards, and mosquito netting. Along with these items, they needed some picks, shovels, axes, hatchets, stout knives, rifles, ammunition and a compass. Snow glasses were considered a necessity. It would take three days to get all the supplies loaded.

Charles and Rachel were finally outfitted and ready to leave. They felt remorse at leaving their good friend Martha with whom their friendship had really grown during this time. Martha said, "Let's please try to keep in touch."

The last leg of their trip took them up through the Yukon and then into Alaska. The sights were unbelievable and they were awestruck more than ever being bored.

When they finally reached Reuben and family, they knew their lives had been and would be forever changed.

Six

Charles and Reuben had discussed financial arrangements and how to set up any claim that might be filed. They had no idea if Reuben would get lucky before Charles arrived. It was a relief to know that he was already a partner and some gold had been found.

Rachel liked the arrangement Dora had set up. She had worried that she would not be able to carry her own weight in panning for gold. She knew, though, that she could cook and wash clothes.

One day, while the men were downstream a ways, Rebekah was trying to pry open a can that held the flour. For some reason, she couldn't get the right grip on it. She had seen Dora use a knife in a similar situation. As she was working the lid loose with the sharp knife, it slipped. It pierced her lower leg and she screamed. Dora almost fainted, but knew she had to remain calm. Rachel came running when she heard the screams. She grabbed some clothes she had been washing, when she saw the blood. At that exact moment, a stranger appeared. He was a black man that Dora had never seen before.

He said, "I can help."

Dora said, "Please do."

He immediately went to work. He cleaned the wound, while reassuring Rebekah, he said, "Now this is going to hurt. Are you going to be brave?"

Through her sobs, Rebekah said, "I am always brave."

He then asked Rachel, "Do you have any honey?" She got some without even questioning why he wanted it. After the wound was cleaned he smeared some honey on it and then carefully bandaged it. He explained as he worked, "My name is James. I am in this area looking for some odd jobs. I heard this little girl's screams and thought I might be able to help." He said, when asked about the honey, "I learned a long time ago to use honey on wounds. It helps to heal and keeps out infection." He told them to clean the wound twice a day and put honey on it with a clean cloth covering it. He asked, "What is your name, brave little girl?"

She giggled a little and said, "It is Rebekah."

Dora said, "Please stay until the menfolk return." James agreed, but took himself off to find some firewood for the evening meal. As the meal was being cooked, he talked to Rebekah.

She had seen very few black people. She had acquired her mother's inquisitiveness, too. So, she came right out and asked, "where are you from, how long have you been in Alaska, have you found any gold, are you married, how did you magically appear when we needed help?" She hardly gave him a chance to answer her questions.

The women were cooking for ten prospectors at present. James was impressed with their arrangement.

When Reuben, Charles, and John arrived and learned of what had happened, they were very appreciative. Reuben tried to get some background information out of James, but was no more successful than Rebekah had been.

After the meal, James bid them all farewell. He had another camp that he hoped to make before it got too late. They all thanked him again. Dora gave him some leftover vittles in case he couldn't find the other camp.

Seven

Weeks went by, then months with no big finds. Tempers began to get short. Some of the prospectors left, abandoning their claims. Some died of exhaustion. The rest just kept struggling. The weather was awful until finally spring arrived.

Most of the snow cover had melted. The streams were running full bank with some flooding. It was pretty dangerous to be working in the streams. Each person had another one close by in case of an accidental falling in the creek. The cold water had claimed lives before.

Reuben and Charles were working this one section that was a little tricky. John and his friend were off trying to snare some rabbits for supper. They heard someone yell for help. It sounded like Charles. John started running. He was terrified of what he might find when he reached his father and uncle. After racing through the woods, they reached the creek. Reuben was in the fast-flowing water. Charles was trying to hang on to a tree while holding out a branch for Reuben to grab. John didn't know what to do first—hold onto Charles or to jump in the water to help his father. He yelled to his friend, "Go get help!" His buddy was already on a run. John jumped in the water. He reasoned there was no way he could help his uncle, but he might be able to help his father reach the branch that Charles was holding out to him.

Just as all seemed hopeless, a familiar figure appeared. James had run into the other youngster. He sent him on for more help and to bring back blankets. He headed for the men in trouble. He assessed the situation and realized Charles was in danger of falling in the water, too. James yelled, "Hold on."

Charles said, "I am trying, but I don't think I can hold on to this leaning tree much longer."

"Just let go and work yourself backwards until I can get an arm around you to get you back to solid ground." Charles knew he had to do this, but didn't want to lose what little hope he had of getting Reuben out of the water. James said calmly, "One thing at a time, ok?"

Meanwhile Reuben was weakening and about to lose his grip on the small tree. John was trying to keep his father talking and alert, but he was growing weak also. After getting Charles back onto the bank, James grabbed a young sapling. He pulled it down and crawled hand over hand while it was bending over the water. He finally got it close to where Reuben was. John grabbed onto the tip of the tree and pulled it close enough for his father to reach it. With James' weight holding the bent sapling down, they were able to pull themselves along until they got close to the bank. By this time Charles had gotten some of his strength back and was able to help pull them out of the water.

James worked his way back down off the bent tree. Men started arriving. They wrapped blankets around the wet, freezing men and helped them get back to camp.

When all the excitement was over, they had to wonder how James appeared again when he was needed. They could not thank him enough.

Reuben began to have suspicions and talked them over with Dora. As soon as he spoke them, she knew it had to be. Now she finally understood the odd feeling she had had as a youngster of being drawn to that long ago "James." He was to play a major part in their future survival, as a "rescuer."

They could hardly wait to talk to him. They had a lot of catching up to do. But James had left camp before anyone arose. Dora said, "He will be back. I just know it, because it's preordained."

Eight

Reuben and Charles had extended their claim to include some as yet unexplored creek bed. It was in this area that the accident had occurred. They had built a sophisticated, elevated system to sift more dirt.

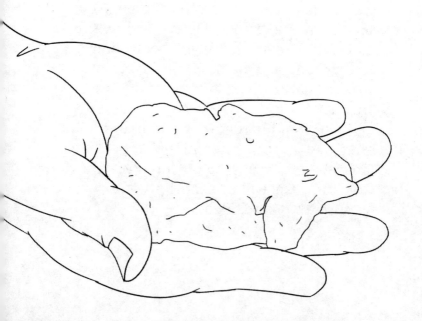

Reuben had thought he saw something in the fast moving water. He had leaned a little too far over and the bank gave way under him. Charles was just far enough away that he was able to get footing. Otherwise, they both would have fallen in and possibly drowned.

By resting up for a day, after their ordeal, the water had slowed a little. They went back to the same area. Dora and Rachel told John, "Don't let them out of your sight." They didn't have to even say that because John had no intention of leaving them.

It was a beautiful, sunshine-filled spring day. Everything just glistened. Birds were singing; majestic eagles were soaring high above the trees.

The men worked diligently. They didn't stop for lunch, just ate a left over hard tack and took sips from the creek.

As Reuben was bending over to get a drink, he again thought he saw something in the water. He called Charles over and said, "Do you see what I think I am seeing?" They stared in amazement and wonder, almost afraid to breathe. Reuben then called John over. He asked, "Will you get in the water and use the small pan to lift up some dirt to run through the big sluice?" When he got into the water, he couldn't believe what he was seeing either. There was not just one large nugget, but almost a pan full. They continued to work until their normal quitting time. They wanted a few hours for this to sink in and to let their emotions settle down.

As suppertime approached, they gathered their tools and bags and quietly walked back to camp. They were afraid to open their mouths—afraid their excitement could not be controlled.

They sat around talking to the men from the other sites, still afraid to say too much. To the surprise of their families, Reuben said he and John would have to make a trip to town. Charles would be staying to work the sluice. Dora would need to help him and Rachel and Rebekah could do the cooking for the day.

After turning in for the night, Reuben whispered to Dora, "I think we have found our fortune." He added, "Don't say a word to anyone." Charles gave the same message to Rachel. Of course the women wanted more information, but knew they had to contain their curiosity for now. It was very hard to fall asleep.

In the morning, Reuben and John started off to town. They were very careful of their words. It was extremely dangerous to strike it rich.

Their "Hope" had come true—the gold they took in was enough to make them rich beyond their wildest dreams.

By the time they got all their business taken care of, it was getting evening. They did not want to stay overnight as they knew the rest would be concerned for their safety. Traveling back to camp as rich men had a different feel to it. They had purchased some fresh-ground coffee and some hard candy, two things they thought would bring pleasure to all of them.

By the time they got back, everyone was on pins and needles. Dora told Rebekah, "Your dad and John have gone into town to have some nuggets assayed."

She asked quietly, "Does that mean we are going to be rich?"

Dora said, "Yes, it looks like our dreams have come true." She was so excited, she could hardly contain herself. She was jumping up and down before they even got off the mules.

While enjoying the fresh-brewed coffee and sucking on peppermint sticks, they discussed their next step. Should they stay and become even richer or should they sell their claim, should they return home, should they set up a business in town, or just what? They decided not to make any decisions until considering all the options.

Nine

After weighing all their options, Charles and Rachel decided they wanted to start a hotel in a nearby town that was just starting to grow. They also decided to write to Martha, the woman that had been so helpful to them. It was their hope that she would be willing to come and help them run the hotel. They would keep a quarter interest in the claim.

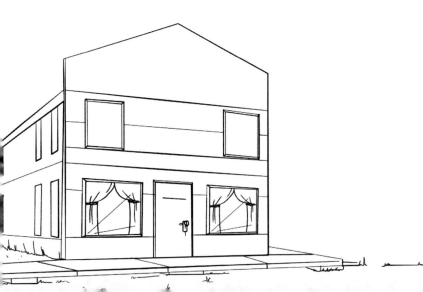

Reuben and Dora decided to keep working as if they were not rich. It wasn't because they were greedy, but rather they felt when the right decision was ready to be made, it would be clear to them. And, besides, "Hope" seemed like home.

Things went very smoothly throughout another year.

Charles and Rachel's hotel was built and doing a booming business. They had named it Hotel Hope. Martha had indeed been more than happy to make the move there. She was a godsend.

Hope just kept supplying gold. The area had become very crowded. Some prospectors were lucky and some were not, just as it had been from the beginning.

James happened by one evening. He had been over at Rabbit Creek when he heard of their big find.

Reuben point blank asked, "Did you travel up secretly from the south?" This took James by total surprise. He was tempted to evade the question or to lie. His gut feeling told him these were good people and he should be honest with them.

Before he could answer, Reuben explained why he had asked.

Dora said, "I wanted to meet you and Ruby so badly. I felt such an attachment to the two of you. I guess it was a premonition of what you would mean to us later in life."

James was overwhelmed. "How could circumstances put me in this same place as my short-time friend, thousands of miles away and so many years having gone by. How could it be that I was near when you and your daughter needed help?"

He had to agree with Dora, "It just must have been supposed to happen this way."

They caught up on the news of what had happened to each of them. James remembered Rachel as being a bundle of energy and how kind she was to Ruby. Reuben asked, "What had happened to her?" James said, "She was placed with a family in New York. She received her education at a fine school. The last I heard from her, she is doing well and still has not married." He added, "I can't wait to tell her about this."

Reuben let Dora tell James what they had decided. Dora began by saying, "James, there aren't any words to tell you how much we appreciate you being here when those emergencies occurred. We have decided to give you a quarter interest in our claim. We also want you to be in charge of Hope. We've decided to move into town near Charles and Rachel. Reuben wants to open a livery/blacksmith shop and I want to start a school."

Again James was overwhelmed. He didn't know what to say. After considering all that he had just been told, he said, "I cannot accept the ownership share. Even though most of us are treated pretty much the same as white men, there are some who still do not like us. I don't want any of these people to make trouble for you."

Reuben reassured James by saying, "No matter your color, there will always be hate and discord to deal with." So James semi-reluctantly accepted the offer.

It was decided they would go into town the next day and draw up all the papers. Another chapter in their lives was being closed.

Ten

As they were traveling to town, with Reuben and John in the buckboard, it slid and a wheel broke. Reuben was thrown off and knocked unconscious. John got thrown off and the buckboard was half lying on him. Rebekah and Dora were riding the mules. James was on his mule when he saw it happen. Rebekah cried out

and Dora flew off her mule and rushed to Reuben. He was breathing and nothing seemed broken. James was already working on getting the buckboard braced so as not to do anymore damage to John. Rebekah was crying but trying to keep calm. John was trying to be brave but couldn't stop the tears from flowing down his cheeks. It appeared the buckboard was lying right on his upper leg. James said, "Dora, let's try to roll this rock close to the buckboard." And to Rebekah, he said, "Look for anything we can use as a lever." When they got the rock by the buckboard, Dora used the iron bar that Rebekah had found to help raise the wagon while James tugged and shoved the rock until he finally got it under one corner. James was then able to pull John out. His leg was badly injured. Rebekah had kept going to her father, talking and crying.

Two spokes were broken on the wheel. There was no way of putting it back on, even temporarily. Dora and Rebekah would have to go the rest of the way into town, get someone to bring back a wheel, and get John to town.

Reuben had come to and seemed to have no injuries. He and James worked to keep John comfortable and warm, who kept going into and out of consciousness, probably from the pain, but they just did not know. Once again, Reuben knew that without James being there, the situation would have been so much worse. How could he ever let him know what his presence meant to them? There were no words.

By the time the wheel had been brought, put on the wagon and John loaded, it was getting dark and very cold. Reuben was still a little woozy, but kept working right along with James to get the buckboard fixed. He did consent to riding in the wagon so he could keep a close eye on John's condition.

It was very late when they finally got into town. The family was all anxiously waiting for them at the hotel. Miraculously, John's leg was not broken, but it did have a very deep cut, huge bruises and many abrasions. The doctor had treated and bandaged it and told them, "Do not let him stand on it for three days." That would give the deep cut a chance to heal. The doctor did not tell them how to tend the wound, but Dora remembered what James had told them to do with Rebekah's wound for it to heal cleanly. They bought a gallon of honey at the general store. Dora, too, realized once more what James had meant to their family.

The next day all the papers were completed at the bank. The owner tried to dissuade them from turning over a quarter share of the claim to James and making him the overseer. He just wanted them to be aware there could be problems down the road. Reuben said, "I am sure whatever befalls James, he will be able to handle it."

The time in town gave them the opportunity they needed to find a location for the livery business and to decide whether to buy an existing home or build a new one. There was already a school in the works. Dora helped by ordering some books and buying benches for it.

When the doctor checked John's leg, he was surprised at how it was healing.

"A good friend told me to use honey on wounds to help them heal and keep out infection, so that's how I've been treating it," Dora said. The doctor was skeptical, but could not deny that the wound was healing cleanly.

They made ready for their last trip to Hope. Arrangements had been made to stay at the hotel while their house was being built.

James had decided he was going to need some help working the sluice. He had wired a friend at Rabbit Creek to see if he would be willing to work for him. His friend, whose name was George, wired back that he would be there in two days.

The move to town was pretty emotional for Reuben and his family. This place called Hope had been their life for the last few years. Dora said, "I feel like we are leaving a part of our heart and soul here."

"Well, we can come back anytime," Reuben said. But they all knew it would never be the same.

Eleven

The Taylors, James, and the Hope Hotel all prospered over the next few years. The town was booming.

In 1900, Reuben decided they should go back home. He was beginning to feel his age. He wanted to see their old home. He wanted his children to have their children know where he had grown up. He knew that he had lived the better part of his life.

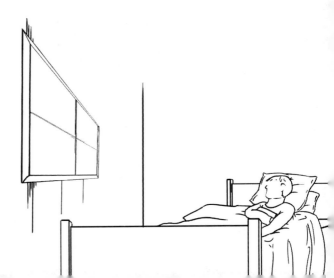

Before they could discuss this with Charles and Rachel, Charles said to Reuben, "We have been thinking of going back home."

Reuben was completely stunned. He said to Charles, "We have thought the same. Again our minds have run together."

Everyone was filled with excitement and anticipation. That is, all but James. He hated to see them go. The bond between Reuben and him was very strong. Once more, they made plans to see each other again at some point in time.

The business deals were closed. James bought out Reuben's shares in the claim. Hotel Hope was taken over by Martha. The livery/blacksmith shop was sold. The fellow that bought the shop also bought their house. Arrangements were finally complete and tickets bought for the trip home.

They had not realized what a tug of war their emotions would go through. They couldn't wait to be on their way but yet hated to leave.

They traveled by stagecoach part way and then by train the rest of the way. It was a very long, strenuous trip.

Dora was very concerned about Reuben. He seemed so pale and drained—like his life was seeping out of him. She spoke of her worries to Rachel. They decided he might feel better if they stopped their travels for a couple of days. Rachel and Charles thought Reuben would accept this idea better if they mentioned that they needed a rest.

They got off the train in Chicago. They were directed to a hotel near the station.

During the evening meal, Reuben passed out. A doctor was summoned. When the examination was over, he said, "This man needs to go to the hospital so I can schedule some tests." It took over three days to evaluate the results of the tests.

The doctor then told them, "Reuben has a very weak heart and a serious lung problem. He will need a long rest with medical care."

A wire was sent to James notifying him of Reuben's condition and of where they were staying.

It was decided they would make arrangements for a long stay at the hotel. Charles would take control of their finances.

"I'm going to look for a job. I can't just sit around," said John. None of them were used to being idle.

As the days went by, Rebekah was spending more and more time at the hospital. She picked up different things from the nurses. She asked one of them, "Can I work alongside you to help take care of my pa?" The nurse was more than glad to have her help. She had seen that Rebekah had a natural feel for tending the sick. Not everyone had this ability.

Dora had made sure both John and Rebekah were educated. She had learned to read, write and do her numbers while she was with her father in his store. Their inherited curiosity gave them incentive to learn. These assets helped them both to obtain jobs. Although Rebekah's was not a paid job at the hospital, it gave her valuable training. John got a job right in the hotel. They had him assist the desk clerk. When they felt he could handle the job alone, he was promoted to night desk clerk.

Reuben had good days and bad. He was recovering, but it was a slow process. Charles was spending a lot of time at a Gentlemen's Club. The discussions were sometimes very heated, especially when it focused on politics. Dora and Rachel spent their time helping out at the primary school. They also spent a lot of time with Reuben and visiting other patients in the hospital.

John loved everything about his job. The people he signed in became personal to him. He could call each one by name and what room they were staying in and for how long.

One day a family named Greene checked in to the hotel, while John was on duty. They were from Virginia and had come to Chicago to check out a prestigious medical school for their son to attend. The family consisted of William, the father,

Yvonne, the mother, Adam, the son, and Elizabeth, the most beautiful girl John had ever seen. He fell in love on the spot.

The families formed a bond right away. The Greenes were fascinated with the tales Charles told of their adventures. Charles and the rest were starving for information from that part of the country.

Twelve

The days passed into weeks, then months and years. Finally a decision had to be made about their future.

John and Elizabeth were planning to marry. Reuben was much improved. Charles was thinking of running for public office. Rebekah was going to nursing school. Dora and Rachel still spent much of their time volunteering at school and hospital.

Charles had signed over the last of his shares in the claim to James. The last he had heard from James, he was thinking of selling out and moving where he would never be cold again. They all chuckled over this.

The votes were cast and it was unanimous—they were staying in Chicago. Reuben, Dora, Rachel, and Charles all requested to have their bodies sent home to Pennsylvania when they passed away. Each one had already made wills and had them recorded. They felt confident that all was taken care of for the future of the children. They also made sure contributions were to be made to hospitals and schools in Chicago and in Pennsylvania.

John talked to his father and uncle about purchasing the hotel that they had come to love.

Arrangements were made to finance this venture. Reuben and Charles had only one requirement. The name of it was to be changed to Hotel Hope.

After John and Elizabeth married, the mortgage was paid in full by Reuben and Charles. John was overcome with joy. He promised that he would never let them down and his life would continue to reflect their teachings.

Reuben passed away in the spring of 1911 at the age of sixty-four. The family finally completed the journey started eleven years earlier.

So much had changed over the years in their hometown. It was hard to recognize any of the landmarks. The homestead still remained in Reuben and Dora's name. The family plot in the town cemetery was surprisingly well tended.

The townspeople turned out to welcome them. They opened their doors so that the six would have places to stay.

After the funeral, Dora wanted to see their home. A distant cousin of hers managed to get a truck to take them all out to it.

It was sad to see the house so overgrown with brambles and barely visible. She made a promise that she would make a yearly trip to visit the cemetery and to work at getting the house back to being livable.

They said goodbye to their renewed acquaintances and vowed to keep in touch.

Dora could never quite get back to her old self after Reuben's death. She tried to adjust, going about her day-to-day life, but it just was not the same.

When a year had passed, she told the family she was going back home and had decided she would not return to Chicago. This information did not surprise anyone. They had seen her continued sadness and just could not help her.

The family all went back one last time. Arrangements were made for Dora to stay with her cousin and his wife until work could be completed on their old home. She was happy to again have a purpose.

When the family was ready to return to Chicago, she told them the next time they came back, the house would be ready for them.

Thirteen

John and Elizabeth's Hotel Hope prospered. In 1915, Elizabeth gave birth to Sarah; in 1917, Tom was born; and in 1920, Harry was born.

Rebekah married Elizabeth's brother, Adam. He was quite a few years older than her, but their love for each other was destined almost from the first meeting.

Adam practiced medicine in a small town about one hundred miles from Chicago. Rebekah helped out as his nurse. They were blessed with four children—Paul, James, Edward, and Shirley.

By 1921, Charles had retired from his political office. He still enjoyed being in the public eye and voicing his displeasure at some of the shenanigans being pulled by some high-ranking officials.

Charles and Rachel decided to return to Pennsylvania. They knew Dora's health was failing. At age seventy-three, she still maintained her home. It was like she was holding on to it for any of the family who might need or want it.

It was decided that all of the family would make the trip. They did not tell Dora of their plans, hoping to surprise her.

A much bigger entourage made this trip—Charles, Rachel, John, Elizabeth, their three children, Rebekah, Adam, and their four children. The private coach ride was fascinating for the children.

Charles and Rachel had made arrangements to meet Dora in town for dinner before going out to the house. During the meal, the lights flickered and when they came back on the rest of the family were standing there. What a celebration followed! It seemed the whole town was there to be a part of the surprise.

The children loved being at the house. There was so much room to run around and so many explorations to be made. None were ready to leave at the end of their visit. A special attachment had developed between them and their grandmother and the farm.

Sadly, that was the last time they saw Dora. About six months later, she went to sleep and never woke up.

Charles and Rachel had settled in nicely and helped with more work at the farm, especially on the grounds. A pond was built and it seemed to produce its own fish. They really grew and multiplied.

Before Dora died, she had discussed her dreams with Charles and Rachel. It was her hope that at least one of her descendants would want to maintain the farm. Until that time came, she wanted Charles and Rachel to own it. She asked that at the demise of the last one of them would they be sure that the property be given equally to John and Rebekah. They gave her their assurance that her wishes would be carried out.

Fourteen

John, Elizabeth, and family spent a lot of time at the farm. John decided he would learn and teach the children to live off the land.

While Charles was helping John work at planting a garden, he suffered a massive heart attack. John was devastated. He felt it was his fault. How could a garden be worth the life of his dear uncle!

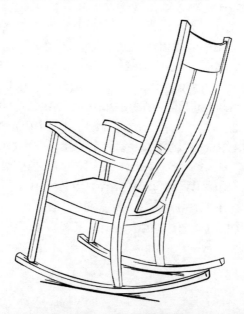

Rebekah, Adam, and their children came for the funeral. While they were all at the farm, Rachel told them of Dora's wishes. She also had tried to make John realize that Charles's death was not his fault. All of the family talked to him, but it did not seem to make any difference.

Upon learning of her mother's wishes, Rebekah seriously discussed with Adam the possibility of their returning to the area. She felt she was being drawn to make this step.

John was also having some serious discussions with Elizabeth. He just didn't feel that he could continue staying there at the present time. Maybe distance would help him accept Charles's death.

Rachel called for a family discussion around the old fireplace. These family discussions had always been the backbone of their decisions. Even the young children were encouraged to participate.

James, Rebekah's second son, spoke up right away and said he wanted this to be his new home. He said his grandma, Dora, had told him that this place was special. She had been sitting in the rocking chair right where his great aunt Rachel was now sitting.

John and Rachel immediately remembered their mother and father relating to them how they had sat in front of this fireplace to discuss the opportunities and dangers of going in search of gold.

They started telling the story of how slaves were hidden in the fireplace, then the decision to make the trip to the gold fields in Alaska, how Reuben and Charles had struck it rich. They also relayed the information about the slave child, James, and how he had played a part in their lives, then how they landed in Chicago, up until the present day. The children were enthralled; even Adam and Elizabeth had never heard all the facts. James said, "I told you this was a special place."

This reminded John and Rebekah of James. John said, "I wonder what became of him."

"How could we have lost touch?" Rebekah asked. They were very remorseful over this lapse.

After careful thought, John decided to go back to Chicago. He had a double reason for this choice. He wanted to return to the hotel business, but he also felt he would have more resources at hand to find James. He felt excited about this decision.

Rebekah and Adam would be returning also, but not permanently. Their plans were to find another doctor for Adam's patients and sell their home, if they could. They would then return to set up a practice in town and get settled in the farmhouse.

John hired a neighbor to take over the manual labor of the farmlands. He was to hire others if he needed help. But all would need to be approved by Rachel.

Fifteen

After returning to Chicago, John started backtracking in trying to find James. His last recollection of any contact was a note of regret after finding out about Reuben's death. John had no idea where to start looking. He decided it best to go to a detective agency. The fellow he went to see thought there must be some thievery involved because white men didn't search for black men unless there had been a

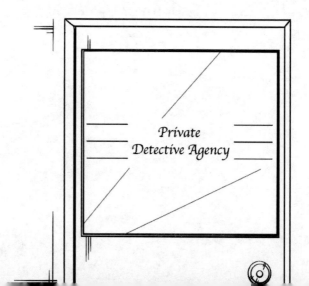

*Private
Detective Agency*

problem. The detective said, "I'll take the case, but you have to be more honest with me. I doubt you are searching for him for the reason you say."

"If I cannot rely on you to trust me, then you are not the person I want. But, I hope you will believe me enough to take this job. I was told you are the very best detective in this area. James is such a special part of our family. We have lost contact due to just being stupid and irresponsible," John said. The detective still wasn't totally convinced, but times were tough and he needed the money.

It took over a month to almost complete the investigation. It would not be totally complete to him until both parties had met. What the detective found really surprised him. James was deceased. He died in 1922. He had no descendents, but he was able to locate Ruby, James' sister. James had stayed in Alaska and his worth had continued to grow. Ruby inherited all of James's wealthy estate. She had married and given birth to five children. Those children gave her twelve grandchildren.

All of Ruby's family had met and loved James. The oldest grandchild was really taken with his great uncle. He was even named James, which created more of a bond. As he grew up, he spent more and more time with his great uncle. He knew all the stories, even to when he and his grandmother Ruby were secreted in a farmhouse in Pennsylvania.

The detective arranged a meeting with Ruby's grandson, James, and John. He did not give many details to James, just enough to let him know that it was important to his client for word about his great uncle.

Before a meeting could be set up, the detective suffered a heart attack and passed away. He was the type of man who kept his knowledge in his head. The company he worked for had no records of his latest case. Once his assignment had been completed, he would have had all the information written up and kept in a safe place. Since the meeting had not taken place, no files had been recorded.

John hit a brick wall when trying to obtain any information on James. It was back to square one.

Before finding another reputable detective, John suffered a terrible loss. Elizabeth fell down a flight of steps. Her back was broken along with multiple other bones. She was paralyzed from her waist down. She was in a coma. John seldom left her side. All of the family spent as much time with her as possible, each one thinking someone close should be there in case she woke from the coma or to be a comfort to John if she passed away. She remained in this state for four weeks. The family was all by her side when she took her last breath.

John lost interest in everything when Elizabeth died. No amount of prodding could bring him out of his depression. In less than two months, he was dead.

The two deaths had a terrible impact on the whole family. Rachel, who was over seventy-five, could not deal with these losses. Her health was quickly deteriorating.

John and Elizabeth were both buried alongside Reuben, Dora, and Charles. After John's funeral, Rachel called for a family discussion. Decisions had to be made regarding the homestead. Rebekah and Adam had not been able to move back as quickly as they had hoped. The foreman John had hired was having a hard time getting good workers. Money was being made quicker up north in factories.

Rachel felt she had no other recourse but to sell the homestead and hope it would eventually end up back in one of the family member's hands.

All of them were so saddened by this turn of events. It was like their whole existence was meaningless. The saddest of all was James. He remembered how he had felt his grandmother's presence and knowing she wanted him to stay in this house. He said, "If I can't call this place 'home,' I'm going as far away as I possibly can go." He ran away, lied about his age, which was actually fifteen, and joined the Army.

Sixteen

Different families tried to make a go of the farm, but just could not do it. Finally, in 1940, the Nelson family purchased it. For some reason, everything seemed to click. Some of the farmland was leased out to a neighboring farmer. Mr. Nelson had a good job with a grocery chain. Mrs. Nelson was expecting her first child. They loved the big house and especially the big fireplace in the basement.

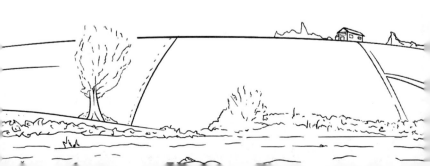

Time passed and the couple had a son and a daughter. World War II was a very bad time for the family. The rationing took its toll on Mr. Nelson's job. He was deaf in one ear, which made him ineligible for the service. Mrs. Nelson helped out with the local Red Cross. They were very thankful to be able to have a garden and provide canned fruits and vegetables for their small family. They were pretty well self-sufficient, but they sure did miss their sweet tea.

After the war ended and the children had grown up and married, the couple thought of selling the farm and moving closer to town. They kept discussing it, but just hated the thought of leaving that beautiful place and moving into something without that big basement and fireplace. Then the grandchildren started coming along. That is when they knew for sure that house was their home for the rest of their lives. So many great memories and daily joys watching the grandkids grow.

During this period of time, a young black family had bought some of the original acreage. Some people were not always friendly to other races, so they pretty much stayed to themselves.

They knew of the local Underground Railroad connection and that a couple of their ancestors had passed through the area. Another bit of information that was part of the tales was that a precious nugget had been brought from Africa and successfully hidden from the slave owners. As the story went, the nugget had been hidden in the fireplace where they were secreted. This way there would always be a place they could return to and begin to build on this small nugget of hope.

The young children, named Ruby and James, after their ancestors, would sneak into the Nelson farmhouse when they thought no one was home or sometimes at night. They meant no harm, just wanted to see if the tales were true.

Seventeen

After the Nelson family attained the information through their investigation of the golden glow, some of the things began to make sense. They decided to invite the father, Charles, and his wife, along with their children, Ruby and James over to openly check out the fireplace.

They were told then of the strange, golden glow. No further evidence could be found in or around the fireplace, but a strong friendship had been formed between the two families.

After going back over the deeds, the Nelsons decided that the best way to end this phenomenon would be to locate some of the original family. The deeds showed the family was Taylor and a connection with Chicago was indicated. A trip was made to Chicago to begin their search. In the newspaper archives, they found stories of the well-known family. The latest descendants were found to be living in Baltimore, not one hundred fifty miles from the original farm.

After contacting Reuben Taylor, who was chairman of the board of a very large nursing home facility, a meeting was scheduled.

Reuben, who knew of some of his past, was totally stunned. He wanted to wait until all information was processed before he got in touch with other family members. It seemed his family's life had finally come full circle.

After the first meeting, all living members of both families were contacted. When his great-uncle, James, was contacted, he was probably the happiest of all. He had always felt the farm was a special place. What a great reunion they had. Friendships were forged. Years and years of memories were recalled. The Nelson family was real excited to be a part of all this history.

James and Ruby were so happy to be made to feel as if they were part of this great family. Their friendship with the Nelson kids was one of the best things that they could ever imagine. Sitting around the big fireplace, they began to wonder—was there really a nugget, or was it an intangible piece of "Hope" to sustain them for whatever might happen and to bring them all together again?

As a footnote: Ann, one of Reuben's granddaughters, caught the eye of Allen, and he was immediately smitten. But that is another story.